DANBI's
Favorite Day

by
Anna Kim

VIKING

To Umma and Appa,
who showed me to never give up

VIKING

An imprint of Penguin Random House LLC, New York

First published in the United States of America by Viking, an imprint of Penguin Random House LLC, 2023

Viking & colophon are registered trademarks of Penguin Random House LLC.

Visit us online at penguinrandomhouse.com.

Library of Congress Cataloging-in-Publication Data is available.

ISBN 9780451478931

Special Markets ISBN 9780593692189 Not for resale

1 3 5 7 9 10 8 6 4 2

RRD

Text set in LTC Kennerley Pro   Manufactured in China

The art was created on watercolor paper using graphite, ink, colored pencil, and watercolor, and finished digitally.

This Imagination Library edition is published by Penguin Young Readers, a division of Penguin Random House LLC, exclusively for Dolly Parton's Imagination Library, a not-for-profit program designed to inspire a love of reading and learning, sponsored in part by The Dollywood Foundation. Penguin's trade editions of this work are available wherever books are sold.

I've got butterflies in my tummy.
My favorite day of the year is coming up,
and I have SO MUCH to do.

"I'm having a Children's Day party, and you're ALL invited!"

"What's that?" asked Nelly.

"Back in Korea, it's the day all your wishes come true!"

"Like your birthday, or Halloween?" asked Maia.

"Even better than that! There's gonna be kites and magic castles. We'll see tigers, ride trains, and eat thousands of chocolate chip cookies!"

"That's baloney!" said David.

"What do you mean, castles and tigers?" Mommy gasped.

"Magic tricks and pony rides, too," I declared, "and they ONLY eat chocolate chip cookies!"

"Oh, Danbi, not this year, honey. Mommy and Daddy have to work at the store."

"But, Mommy! I promised everyone!"

"Sweetie," Mommy said. "Children's Day is not just about things; it's about celebrating all the children on Earth who will one day lead the world. Let's have a lovely party behind the deli. I think your friends will love the rice cakes, too."

On the morning of the party, after a nice breakfast . . .

"Danbi, eat your seaweed soup!"

"Pancakes, too!"

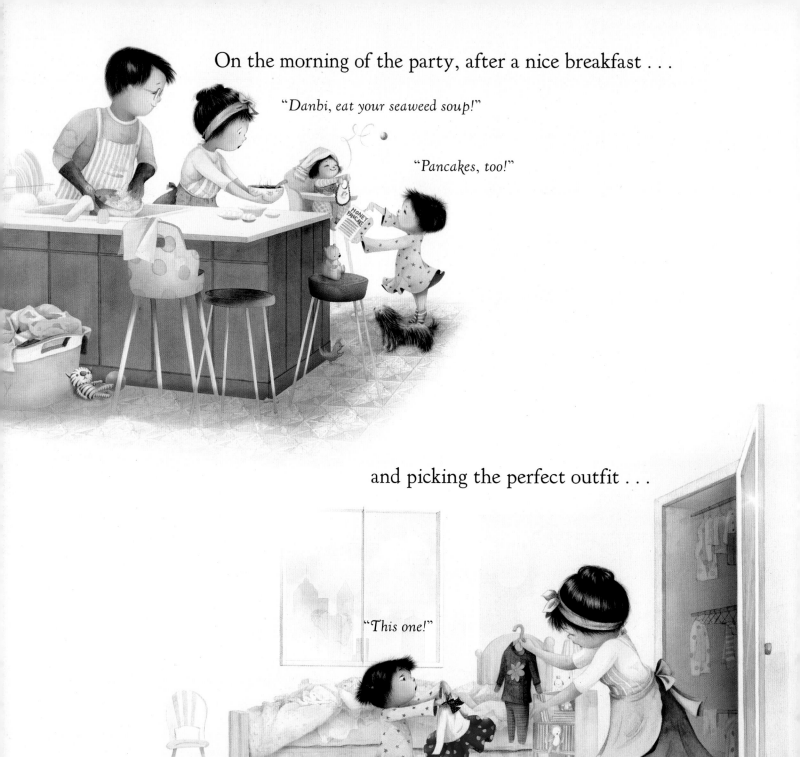

and picking the perfect outfit . . .

"This one!"

we were on our way!

"*Danbi, they say it may rain today.
Let's set up inside the deli.*"

"*But, Mommy,
it's sunny! I want
a picnic!*"

Mommy brought out colored chalks.
Daddy set up a big table.
I put out streamers, fruits, and flow-
ers; and I swept, wiped, cleaned,
and mopped.

I hopped around the table and tied big balloons. It was perfect.

One by one, my friends arrived.
A pink chalk for Nelly,

a green one for Maia,

a blue and a red for
Arjun and David.

We turned up the music!

We drew! We danced! We rocked!

CHA CHA BOOGIE WOOGIE BOOM BOOM
CHA CHA BOOGIE WOOGIE BOOM BOOM

I was the perfect hostess.

BA-BANG!

The sky roared, and wind
tore through the alley.

It was just as Mommy said.

Mommy spoke to me gently:
"Everyone is waiting for you.
Are you going to let some rain
spoil your party?"
I shook my head side to side.

"Your friends can have anything
they want in the deli. How about
helping them pick something?"

Our treasure hunt was over in two minutes.

"That's it?" asked David. "Now what?"

"What about the train and tigers?" asked Maia.

"I want to go home," said Arjun.

I had to save my party.

"Who wants the best
sandwich in town?"
I asked.

"Nobody," said David.

I took a deep breath and gave it my best shot:
peanut butter, peppers, bacon, jelly, sesame seeds . . .

SWOOSH
WOOSH

SPRINKLE
SPRINKLE

. . . and a mountain of whipped cream!
It swelled. It ballooned.
And for a special touch, a spoonful of
thick red cherry syrup!

"It's A VOLCANO!" Arjun cried.

Nelly and Maia wanted to make something, too!

"Go for it!" I said.

We searched far and wide . . .

high and low, for the most mouthwatering, lip-smacking,
finger-licking stuff we could find and got to work.

Uh-oh! I had to show everyone how it's done.

Line up and stack up!

Bulgogi, ham, cheese, salsa, gummy bears, curry, kimchi, tofu, marshmallows, and meatballs . . .

"Hey! It's a train!"
David cried.

A sandwich train! *CHOO-CHOO!*

Together we could do so much.

I felt a tickle in my belly. A pink, happy tickle.

The sunlight pierced the clouds, and our street
lit up like a blaze of fire.

"C'mon everyone!" I jumped. "Let's go outside!"
Kids in the neighborhood waved hello, and I waved back. "Welcome to Children's Day!"

Mommy lifted the honey rice cake from the steamer and brought out freshly baked chocolate chip cookies from the oven.

"Mommy's rainbow cake! The BEST in the world."
I showed everyone how I eat it:
"With all ten fingers!"

Fluffy, chewy, squishy, springy, sticky, soft, and sweet.

It was a hit.

At the end of the day, Daddy opened a new box of chalk.
We drew a mural and hopped in the puddles.
Waterdrops bounced like jewels in the sun.

I felt that pink tickle again,
and it turned to gold.

We were the children of the world.

That night, I gulped down Mommy's seaweed soup to the last drop.

"Danbi." Mommy smiled. "You gave your friends a wonderful day."
And I said, "It was the best! I'm gonna remember this day forever."

Today was not my birthday.
It was not Halloween.
It was about being together.
It was my Children's Day.